The Adventures Of

SASSY AND ROWDY

Episode 3

Danger in the Big Thicket

By Marvin E. Jones

Illustrated By

Tim Czarnecki

EAKIN PRESS   ★   **Austin, Texas**

ISBN 0-89015-752-9

Library of Congress Cataloging-in-Publication Data

Jones, Marvin E.
　　Danger in the Big Thicket / Marvin E. Jones : illustrations by Tim Czarnecki.
　　　p.　　cm. — (The Adventures of Sassy and Rowdy Krackers : episode 3)
　　Summary: Young raccoons Sassy and Rowdy join the magical inhabitants of
the Enchanted Valley in a final struggle for survival against the impending danger
that threatens the safety of all in the forest.
　　ISBN 0-89015-752-9 : $9.95
　　[1. Raccoons — Fiction. 2. Fantasy.]　I. Czarnecki, Tim, ill.　II. Title.　III.
Series: Jones, Marvin E. Adventures of Sassy and Rowdy Krackers : episode 3.
PZ7.J7219Th　1988
[Fic] — dc20　　　　　　　　　　　　　　　　　　　　　　89-72180
　　　　　　　　　　　　　　　　　　　　　　　　　　　　　　CIP

This book is dedicated to four very special people:
my daughters-in-law,
Shawna, Tammy, Debbie, and Tina.

Contents

Preface

Fairy tales, legends, and myths have entertained children throughout the ages. Families have joined together by candlelight while these tales unfolded fantasies in their minds.

The Adventures of Sassy and Rowdy series, written and dedicated to the entertainment of children, embraces modern times with fantasy and science fiction to promote wholesome family values. The entire story unfolds in three books: Episode 1, *The Enchanted Valley*; Episode 2, *Gory Gary Strikes Back*; and Episode 3, *Danger in the Big Thicket*.

It is hoped you will take time to join your family in reading them together. Enjoy the delightful experience of a family sharing love and laughter as you follow Rowdy and Sassy's adventures in the world of fantasy.

Summary from Episode 1

One early spring the human family moved into the old, abandoned farmhouse at the edge of the Big Thicket. There was Uncle Jim, the editor of a small-town newspaper, with his two nephews, Tommy and Kevin, and their sister, Donna. With them were their two dogs, Charles and Samantha, and their farm hand, Pete.

The dogs soon met and quickly became friends with the raccoon family: the father, Sebastian, and his twin children, Sassy and Rowdy Krackers. Charles and Samantha helped free Sassy and Rowdy from one of Hunter John's traps.

The two young raccoons repaid Charles and Samantha's kindness by saving Kevin from flood waters after a tremendous storm. While saving Kevin, they were swept out into the Great River on a makeshift raft. The three escaped doom when they were rescued by Willard, the Wizard Lizard of the Enchanted Valley.

In the Enchanted Valley they met Boo, a cross-eyed bat who was Willard's assistant. Rowdy and Boo's personalities conflicted at first meeting, but they became good friends as time passed.

While they were in the Enchanted Valley, Kevin, Sassy, and Rowdy also met the six-inch-tall King Benjamin, ruler of the Sagittarians.

A colony of the Sagittarians had come to this world several thousand years ago from a planet whose sun was exploding. The colony of Sagittarians consisted of little people about six inches in height and other very small creatures. They had settled in seclusion in the vast wilderness of the Big Thicket and had developed the Enchanted Valley.

Kevin received a special ring from King Benjamin that enabled him and his brother and sister to talk with and understand the animal kingdom. Kevin was taught how to use the ring to contact the Enchanted Kingdom, if necessary. He was also told that the ring was connected to the mysterious and powerful Oracle in the Enchanted Kingdom. It had many additional powers, but Kevin was warned not to attempt to use or experiment with those powers.

Upon returning to their own homes Kevin's brother, Tommy, and Rowdy became curious about the power of the ring. They experimented with it and saw amazing results: they called up the spirit of the Great Jumpin' Jehoshaphats, a curious-looking creature that had the legs of a kangaroo, the body of a fat horse, and the neck and head of a dragon. This fire-breathing, high-jumping creature they named Gee.

King Benjamin, on his high-speed air scooter, called to help them to decide what to do with this most interesting creature. During this visit he learned that when they were very small, Sassy and Rowdy's mother had been captured by Hunter John. The king became very fond of the young raccoons and was touched by their longing to find their mother, Amanda.

Returning to his kingdom, the king ordered his subjects on an all-out search for Amanda. He also enlisted the aid of a Chinese soothsayer, Danny Wo.

Through their combined efforts they located Amanda in an institution for the study of animal behavior in Dallas. She and over one hundred other animals had been leased by the institution from Hunter John. When they located Amanda they discovered that the experiments were over. She and all the other animals were being returned to Hunter John's farm that same night. The hunter had hired an evil man named Gory Gary to slay and skin the one hundred animals being brought back, plus over one hundred other animals the hunter had caged in his barn.

Being forbidden by Sagittarian law from directly interfering in the human or animal population of this world, the king planned, advised and assisted the children, their farm hand, and the animal population of the forest with the saving of Amanda and over two hundred other animals. The rescue was successful in freeing all the animals and reuniting Amanda with her family.

One of the animals saved was a small girl raccoon, named Patches because her fur was splotched in a patchwork of brown and gray. Patches had been orphaned when she was very small and had no family or home to return to, so the raccoon family adopted her and took her to live with them.

The evil animal skinner, Gory Gary, had gotten a glimpse of the six-inch king, the Chinese soothsayer, Pete, and Gee. He swore revenge on them and the raccoon family for setting the animals free.

Summary from Episode 2

On a lovely spring day the young raccoons, Sassy, Rowdy and Patches, visited the children at the old farm. Kevin was playing his guitar while Tommy accompanied him on the drums. Rowdy and the girl raccoons were so impressed that they wanted to learn to play the instruments. Pete suggested that his cousin could make small instruments for them.

They all went to town to propose the idea to his cousin. While there, they overheard their old enemy, Gory Gary, getting permits for animal traps from Ranger Kenneth.

The word was soon passed around the forest, and Sebastian called a meeting of all the animal kingdom. It was arranged that the birds would watch where the traps were placed and warn the animals. The animals then safely sprung the traps, foiling Gory Gary's attempts to trap them.

Constantly finding empty but sprung traps frustrated Gary. He convinced Hunter John to help him alter the traps illegally and reset them at night.

The beings from King Benjamin's world who were patrolling learned of this and reported to the king. The king passed the word to Sebastian to find a way to keep the animals together and safe. Sebastian came up with an idea. Sassy, Rowdy, and Patches gave a concert for the animals at Digger Doug's cavern. They had received their tiny musical instruments and had quickly become proficient at playing them.

The king made Ranger Kenneth aware of Gary's illegal traps. That resulted in Gary and John being arrested.

After the concert, Rowdy and Kadiddle Hopper Rabbit planned a prank on Sassy and Patches. The prank backfired when they all encountered the Who-Done-Gotcha monster. After recovering from their fright, they discovered that the big, ugly creature was very lonely and was not a threat to them. His name was Woosie, and he had been separated from his parents for many years.

The young raccoons decided King Benjamin could find Woosie's parents since he had located their mother. They hid Woosie in Fangs' cave and shared their idea with the children. All gathered at the cave and Kevin contacted King Benjamin. Since the king's messengers were reporting all activities in the forest, he was already working on the problem. The king revealed that eleven other colonies of his people had also escaped from their exploding world and had set up kingdoms just as he and the Sagittarians had. King Benjamin's cousin, King Brandon, had settled on an island southeast of this continent. Woosie's parents were found there and were transported to the Enchanted Kingdom for a joyful reunion with Woosie.

King Benjamin also revealed a plan to teach Gary and John a lesson upon their release from jail. With the help of DC Bones, a Bushtron and head scientist of the Enchanted Kingdom, King Benjamin prepared an elaborate plan to frighten the evil Gary and John into leaving the forest animals in peace.

The king's plan involved allowing himself to be captured by Gary and John, then luring them to the Enchanted Valley. There, with the help of DC Bones' reduction guns and the many wonderful beings of the Enchanted Kingdom, the evil ones were thoroughly terrorized and convinced that leaving the animals in peace was to their own best interest.

A happy reunion and celebration was held in the Enchanted Kingdom after the successful completion of their plan. As the celebration was ending, King Benjamin hinted to the children that a threat might be coming to the whole area, affecting them all. He asked for their help if the threat became a reality.

Upon their return to the old farm, the children heard disturbing news from Uncle Jim. He had been meeting with a committee in Austin and disclosed to the children that unwelcome changes might be coming to the Big Thicket.

Let us rejoin our story now for the final episode, in the first series, of the *Adventures of Sassy and Rowdy*.

Chapter 1

Fireworks for Rowdy

It was early summer, and the small town just outside the Big Thicket was preparing for the Fourth of July celebration.

Rowdy, Sassy, and Patches were visiting the children at the old farm. As the children and raccoons played about the barn, they heard Pete call to them, "It is time to go to town now." Climbing into Pete's old pickup, they bumped down the country road that led to town.

As they approached the small town, Tommy exclaimed, "Wow! Neat! Look, Kevin!"

"Yeah," said Kevin, "I see."

Sassy asked, "What do you see?"

Tommy pointed at a large fireworks stand on the side of the road and asked Pete, "Can we stop and buy some fireworks?"

"Sure," replied Pete as he pulled over to the beautifully colored fireworks stand.

With the raccoons on their shoulders, the children purchased an assortment of firecrackers, Roman candles, and other delightful items.

Getting back into the truck, Rowdy examined a package of firecrackers and asked, "What are those things you have?"

1

"Well," said Tommy, "those are firecrackers."

"What do they do?" asked Rowdy.

"You light the fuse here, and they go BANG!"

Rowdy's eyes widened in curiosity as he said, "Show me, Tommy."

"When we get back home, I will."

Pete and the children finished shopping for various items they needed, then returned to their home.

"Now," said Rowdy, "show me how the firecrackers work."

The children sat down and unraveled a package of firecrackers. Tommy lit a punk light stick, then said to Rowdy, "You touch the lit end of this punk stick to the long fuse on the end of the firecracker, like this."

Rowdy watched the fuse burning on the firecracker, then suddenly, without warning, came a loud BANG! Rowdy squealed in delight, "Let me do it!"

For the next hour or so they took turns lighting and popping the firecrackers.

As the sun set and darkness gathered, Kevin said,

"Watch this," and he lit a huge skyrocket. The skyrocket took off with a sudden thrust of power, soared high in the sky, and exploded into brilliant, beautiful colors and stars. The little raccoons watched with amazement.

After shooting off several kinds of beautiful fireworks, it was time for the raccoons to return to their home in the old hickory. As they prepared to depart on the flying air scooter King Benjamin had given them, Tommy said, "Here, Rowdy, you can have some of these packs of firecrackers, but be very careful with them in the forest, so that you don't start a fire."

Stuffing the packages of firecrackers and a small box of matches into his pocket, Rowdy fired up the air scooter and zoomed away with Sassy and Patches riding behind him.

Back at the old hickory, Rowdy snuggled down in his bed as wonderful visions danced through his mind of all the terrific pranks he could play with the firecrackers.

Let's see, he thought, *I could light one and drop it down Gabby Gopher's hole and I'll bet old Gabby would come leaping out! Oh no, it might pop before he got out of the hole and it might hurt him. Oh, I know what I'll do! I will light a whole pack just outside Lonesome Skunk's den and he will get all excited and come rushing out! Oh, my goodness, no, he probably would be so excited he would be spraying that stinky skunk juice everywhere and some of it might even get on me. Whew! That would be awful!*

Rowdy's mind raced on in endless daydreaming about the various fun ways he could pop the firecrackers, until at last, he fell fast asleep.

Rising early the next morning, Rowdy heard voices outside the old hickory. Looking out the window, he saw his father visiting with Slick, the Weasel Lawyer. As usual, Slick had the book titled *Texas Wildlife Rules and Regulations* tucked under his arm. *Ah,* thought Rowdy, *Slick has been giving me a hard time about my air scooter. This is the perfect opportunity to even the score.*

Taking one firecracker and a match, he crawled out his window and eased out on a limb directly over Slick. Rowdy lit the firecracker and whispered, "Bombs away," as he dropped the little firecracker soundlessly behind Slick. *BANG* went the loud firecracker, and Sebastian and Slick leaped into the air.

Dropping the law book, Slick yelled, "Run, Sebastian, someone's shooting at us!" Both quickly dived into the bushes and peered out cautiously to see where the shot came from.

Sebastian heard Rowdy laughing on the limb above and said, "It's all right, no one is shooting at us. It is just Rowdy, popping firecrackers that the children gave him."

Stomping out of the bushes, Slick angrily said, "Sebastian, you need to do something about that boy!"

"I apologize for Rowdy frightening you, and I will certainly speak to him." Saying goodbye, Slick departed, his anger only slightly calmed.

"Rowdy, come down here at once!" shouted Sebastian.

"Uh-oh," said Rowdy to himself, "Papa sounds angry." He scurried down the trunk of the old hickory, and with an innocent, boyish look on his face, asked, "You want something, Papa?"

Sebastian stood with both hands on his hips, tapping one foot on the ground. "Rowdy, I know you and Slick don't get along, but I want to warn you, son, that you are making a powerful enemy. One of these days it might come home to haunt you."

"Yes, Papa," replied the humbled Rowdy.

As Sebastian entered the old hickory, Sassy and Patches bounded out into the yard and approached Rowdy. They both giggled as Sassy said, "You shouldn't have done that, Rowdy, but did you see how high old Slick jumped?"

Giggling along with the girls, Rowdy replied, "Yes, and did you see how high Papa jumped, and how fast he ducked into the bushes? I have never seen him move that fast before!"

Sebastian was standing just inside the old hickory's door, listening to the young raccoons giggle and discuss what had happened. As he stood there in silence, he began to chuckle.

Amanda asked, "What are you chuckling about?"

"Oh, Mother, for a minute I was remembering what it is like to be a boy," replied Sebastian.

Out in the yard, Rowdy had an idea. "Let's go find Kadiddle Hopper and go down by the old creek. We can swing out over the water on the grapevines." Agreeing that it was a fine idea, all three little raccoons scurried off to find their friend, Kadiddle Hopper the Rabbit.

After playing and roaming around the forest, they found Kadiddle Hopper at the edge of the meadow, munching on some clover.

"Hi ya, Kadiddle Hopper," said Rowdy.

"Well, howdy," replied the rabbit.

"Want to go with us down to the old creek and swing out over the water on the grapevines?"

"Sure," said Kadiddle Hopper, "that sounds like great fun."

As the hot Texas sun dried the last of the morning dew, the four of them ran off toward the old creek for a morning of adventure.

Chapter 2

Woody the Wanderer

At the old creek, the four little critters found a special thrill in swinging out on a grapevine and dropping into the cool clear water, then swimming back to the bank. Their play was interrupted by the sound of a deep, human voice, singing. As they paused to listen intently, they realized the sound was coming from up the creek a way.

"Let's go see who it is," said Rowdy. The little ones slipped quietly along the creek bank until they came in sight of a large old truck that appeared to have a small house built on the back of it.

A very old, silver-haired human was preparing breakfast by the creek. His eyes were deep blue and sparkled against his gray eyebrows. Most of his wrinkled face was covered by a snow white beard that wiggled as he sang.

"Who's that?" asked Kadiddle Hopper.

"I don't know," replied Rowdy, "I have never seen him before." The four curious little critters crept through the brush until they were only a few feet away from the strange looking human.

The stranger stopped singing and sat in silence for a few moments, then said, "My name is Woody, if you wish to come

on in."

Sassy whispered to Rowdy, "Who is he talking to? I don't see anyone."

The stranger spoke again. "I am talking to the four of you hiding in the bushes."

"Should we run?" whispered Patches.

The stranger said, "Why would you want to run? You have nothing to fear from me."

The four friends boldly ventured out and, standing in front of the stranger, Sassy asked, "Do you understand what we are saying?"

The stranger replied, "I not only understand what you are saying, but I can also hear your thoughts."

As the four carefully looked the stranger over, a sleek, black cat with large, green eyes leaped into his lap.

Petting the cat, the stranger said, "Allow me to introduce us. My friend and companion, the cat, is Pywacket. I am known among my friends as Woody the Wanderer."

Sassy curtsied and said, "I am Sassy Krackers and this is my brother, Rowdy. This is Patches and Kadiddle Hopper."

Rowdy eased forward and asked, "Where do you wander from?"

Woody replied, "I wander from many places and times."

"Oh," said Rowdy, "then where are you wandering to?"

Woody gently stroked Pywacket's head and replied, "I wander from here to there. I wander from back to forth. I wander from up to down. I wander into the future from out of the past. I wander to where I am called from where I have been. I wander to where I am needed from where I was, and then I wander back again. Sometimes I even wander in a circle."

Unable to get a straight answer, the impatient Rowdy exclaimed, "Well, you certainly talk in circles!" Rowdy noticed that the cat had been staring intently at him, so he continued, "Can your friend, the cat, speak? And why is it staring at me?"

Woody answered, "It can speak when it has something to say, and it is studying you to see what there is to see." The cat slid from Woody's lap and eased close to Rowdy, still staring intently at the young raccoon.

"What do you mean?" asked Rowdy. "I am here. That's what it sees."

Woody chuckled a minute, then said, "My little friend, sometimes what you think you see is not what you are seeing, but what one wishes for you to see. Or perhaps what you are seeing is only what you want to see, and not what you should be seeing."

Frowning, Rowdy replied, "The only thing I see is that you are talking in circles again."

"Is not life itself often a circle?" replied Woody. "If one could see where he is going as clearly as he sees where he has been, would he not see that he is often repeating the same things, and is not that like a circle?"

Rowdy pondered for a minute, then replied, "I see you are here, and I see the cat is creeping closer and still staring at me."

"Are you sure we are here? Are you sure you are seeing us as we really are? Perhaps you are only seeing what we wish for you to see."

The confused and angry Rowdy snapped, "I am sure that I see you and I am sure that if your cat creeps any closer to

stare at me, the only thing it is going to see is stars, when my
fist bounces off the end of its nose!"

Having drawn very close to Rowdy, the cat spoke, "I am
Pywacket. I mean you no harm. I only wish to make certain
that you are what you appear to be."

With his hands on his hips, Rowdy stared the cat straight
in the eyes and replied, "What you see is what I am. I cannot
be seen as anything other than what you are seeing. Oh, my
gosh, now you've got me talking that ridiculous way!"

Woody chuckled again and said, "Rowdy, the power of
illusion can be great, and can make you believe that you are
seeing what is not there."

"That's hogwash! I don't believe that!" replied Rowdy.
"I cannot see what is not there."

"Very well," said Woody, "then behold the power of illusion." Woody reached forward and passed his hand across
Rowdy's nose.

Terrified and astonished, Rowdy watched his nose grow
a foot long. Backing away, holding his enormously long nose
with both hands, Rowdy screamed, "What did you do to me?"

Sassy, Patches, and Kadiddle Hopper stood horrified, unable to speak, as they stared at Rowdy's nose. Woody replied, "I have done nothing to you. You only see what I want you to see, which is not really there."

"You mean," gasped Rowdy, "my nose is not really long?"

"That is correct," answered Woody.

Rowdy rushed back up to Woody. "Well, make it disappear. I don't like it. I don't want it to be there, even if it is not really there!"

"Very well," said Woody. He passed his hand back across Rowdy's nose, and it returned to its original size.

"Whew," said Rowdy, as he felt of his little black nose, "don't you ever do that again!"

Kadiddle Hopper stuttered a moment, then finally managed to ask, "What are you, a witch?"

"I am known by many names and I have taken many forms."

Patches timidly asked, "You mean, you are not a human, and Pywacket is not a cat?"

"That is correct."

Sassy began to sense that the stranger was a friend. She sweetly asked, "Good sir, do you mean us any harm?"

"No," replied Woody, "to the contrary, we are here at the request of a mutual friend, to assist you and the human children against the impending threat to the forest."

"What mutual friend?" asked Sassy.

"King Benjamin, ruler of the Sagittarians," replied Woody.

Still feeling his nose to make sure it was there, Rowdy asked, "King Benjamin sent you?"

"No, he did not send us. He requested our presence in this area."

"Are you part of the Sagittarians?" asked Sassy.

"No, we are not a part of the Sagittarians, or of the other eleven colonies from King Benjamin's world."

"Then are you of this world?" asked Patches.

"No," replied Woody, "we are not of this world. We are strangers and wanderers in your world, and in your time."

Kadiddle Hopper, very puzzled, scratched his head. "You are not of our world? And you are not of our time? And things are not what they appear to be? You are not human? Pywacket is not a cat? Then what *are* you? Where did you come from, and what do you really look like? I tell you, all of this makes my head hurt trying to understand!"

Woody chuckled again. "We are from a galaxy far away. We are known as Illusions. We appear to you in this form, so that you will be comfortable around us. Do you want to see us in our true appearance?"

The little critters huddled close together and replied, "Yes."

"Very well," said Woody, "then behold our true image."

Everyone looked in amazement as Woody and Pywacket transformed into their true form. Each was about one foot tall and had a spider-like body with six hairy legs. In the center of their round, red bodies was one large, blue eye. Extending from the top of their bodies were two antennas. Where the old truck had been standing, now stood a round ball that hovered just about six inches off the ground. It was a sparkling, brilliant, turquoise color.

Staring at the ugly, frightening images of the Illusions, Rowdy shouted, "That's enough! Go back to the way you were!"

Honoring the request, Woody returned to the form of a human, Pywacket to the form of a cat, and the ball to its appearance of a truck. Woody smiled kindly at the four and stated, "My little friends, you may have found our true appearance frightening, but let me assure you, we are quite harmless and our hearts are very good. We have been trapped for some time on your planet, but soon the conditions will be right for us to return to our own world. In the meantime, however, we have wandered about your world in different forms, enjoying the different beings that populate it."

"How do you know King Benjamin?" asked Sassy.

"The beings from our world knew the beings from King Benjamin's world long before their sun exploded. We would have gladly shared our planet with them, but they could not survive in our atmosphere."

"What did you mean when you said you are here to assist us and the human children against a threat to the forest?" asked Rowdy.

Woody gazed at Rowdy a moment before replying, "King Benjamin requested our presence in this area. He feels that our power of illusion might be needed."

Sassy drew closer to Woody and asked, "What is about to threaten our beautiful forest?"

"Human progress," replied Woody.

Rowdy paced back and forth in front of the kindly looking Woody. Putting aside his usual boyish and mischievous nature, he assumed a look of serious concern as he stated, "Several times we have been told that our forest is in danger. Will you please explain what human progress has to do with the safety of our forest?"

The mysterious Woody studied the puzzled looks on their faces, then replied, "King Benjamin has a plan to remove this danger from your forest. He will, at the proper time, explain the danger and what must be done. Now, my little friends, I suggest you leave it in his hands and let it trouble you no longer."

Pywacket leaped back into Woody's lap and said, "It is time to renew our energy."

"Yes, I feel myself growing weak," replied Woody. Rising to his feet, he said, "We must go now."

"Where are you going?" asked Rowdy.

Smiling, Woody answered, "From time to time we must return to our original form, to renew our energy fields. We must go into another dimension and time, return from time and places, back and forth, up and down, around and back, in and out."

"Sorry I asked," snapped Rowdy.

Chuckling, Woody said, "This one must learn patience, Pywacket."

"Yes," replied the cat, "he is a valiant spirit and will be a tremendous force for Good in the animal kingdom, when his patience grows as large as his mouth."

Angered by the cat's words, Rowdy started to move closer. He was stopped by Kadiddle Hopper, who whispered, "Remember what happened to your nose!" Pausing to reflect, Rowdy decided to allow the cat's insult to go unanswered.

Rowdy then asked, "How can we find you?"

Holding the cat in his arms, Woody replied to Rowdy's question. "You will not have to find us. We will seek you out when we are needed." With that statement, Woody and Pywacket climbed into the old truck. As the little critters watched in amazement, the truck changed into a little turquoise ball and in the twinkling of an eye, disappeared into the sky.

Rowdy stood with both hands on his hips, gazing into the sky where the ball vanished. Drawing from an expression he had heard Tommy use to describe unusual people, he exclaimed, "Those are sure two weird dudes!"

"I don't think so," said Sassy. "If King Benjamin has asked them to be here, then they must be good and they will be our friends."

"Yeah," admitted Rowdy, "you are probably right." Then, smiling his little devilish grin, he continued, "I wonder if they could teach me how to do that illusion trick?" The grin

13

14

widened on Rowdy's face and his eyes sparkled with delight as he thought to himself, *Boy, could I ever have some fun with that.*

Kadiddle Hopper strolled up to Rowdy to speak, but Rowdy still had a faraway look in his eyes. The rabbit tapped Rowdy on the shoulder and asked, "Friend, are you still with us, or did you leave with them?"

"Oh, yeah, I'm here," replied Rowdy, coming out of his daydream.

"Well," said Sassy, "let's go home and tell Papa about all of this." They agreed and the little critters scurried away toward the old hickory.

Chapter 3

Uncle Stumpy and Robocoon

Trying to escape the heat, Sebastian had found himself a large, shady place under the old hickory and sat fanning himself. Sassy, Rowdy, and Patches bounded up to him and excitedly related their encounter with Woody the Wanderer.

"Well," said Sebastian, "I guess the forest is full of excitement today, because I have some exciting news to tell you too."

With pure sweetness in her face, Sassy stood clasping her hands in front of her and swayed back and forth while she asked, "What exciting news do you have to tell us, Papa?"

"Your Uncle Stumpy arrived this morning while you were away playing in the forest."

Grabbing each other, Sassy and Rowdy jumped around happily as Rowdy exclaimed, "That's great! I love all the wonderful stories you have told us about Uncle Stumpy."

"Where is he?" asked Sassy.

"He was very weary from his journey home and is napping in the old hickory," replied Sebastian.

"Who is Uncle Stumpy?" timidly asked Patches.

Clapping his hands in delight, Rowdy replied, "He is the most super, neat, and fantastic uncle in all the world. He has sailed the Seven Seas with his old master and has had so many fantastic adventures, and — and — "

"Whoa," interrupted Sebastian, "let's don't overdo it." After a moment, Sebastian continued, "He is my uncle and Sassy and Rowdy's great-uncle. He left the forest many years ago when he was young, to explore the world outside of our forest. While he was down by the coast of Galveston, his leg was injured in a trap. His injury was so serious it resulted in the loss of part of his left leg. An old sailor found him in his crippled condition and, taking pity on him, had a local veterinarian build him a wooden leg. When the old sailor saw him stump around on his peg leg, he named him Stumpy. The old sailor took Stumpy to his boat. They became shipmates and sailed the Seven Seas together."

"Yes," said Rowdy, "and Uncle Stumpy sends us neat stuff from all over the world, whenever he finds an animal that is coming this way." Pulling a small knife with many gadgets on it out of his pocket, Rowdy continued, "He sent me this from a place called China."

"Oh, he sounds wonderful," said Patches. "I can't wait to meet him."

Sebastian chuckled a moment, then said, "Uncle Stumpy is truly a remarkable raccoon. But let me warn you, Patches, he is also probably one of the biggest windjammers you will ever meet."

"I heard that, matey," shouted Uncle Stumpy, standing in the door of the old hickory. "I'll tell you a truth, me and the old master have threatened to make lads walk the plank for lesser statements."

Absolute silence fell over the three little raccoons and Ka-diddle Hopper as they stared at the unusual figure standing in the door. In all the forest there could be few sights to top this colorful character. He was large in size. His brown fur was tinted with streaks of gray, showing his extreme age. He stood erect on his wooden leg, with a small sword strapped to his side. Over his right eye was a large black patch, and he wore a hat similar to that of an olden pirate. While his one good eye was old, it still sparkled with a boyish-like mischievousness.

The silence was broken by Uncle Stumpy, who said, "So this is my great-niece and nephew. They sure be a sight for

sore eyes, or in my case, a sight for a sore eye, ha-ha!" Stretching his arms out toward them, he said, "Come, mateys, and give your old Uncle Stumpy a hug." Sassy and Rowdy dashed over and hugged him. "Well, I'll tell you another truth, these are sure fine looking kids. I'm glad to see they took their looks from their mother and not from a homely, old swabbie like you, Sebastian."

Rowdy looked up at Uncle Stumpy with admiration beaming from his face. He asked, "Would you tell us about some of your adventures?"

"Ah, you be true shipmates after me own heart. Of course, I will share a tale or two with you," replied Uncle Stumpy.

Limping across the yard, he sat down on a log while the young raccoons and Kadiddle Hopper gathered on the ground in front of him. Uncle Stumpy cocked his head to one side and squinted his one good eye at his audience seated in front of him. "Now, let me see, mates, what would you be liking to hear?"

Kadiddle Hopper said, "How did you get that patch over your eye?"

Rearing back and laughing, Uncle Stumpy replied, "Oh, now that's a yarn that will sure enough chill your blood. Do you lads and lasses have the stomach for it?"

Sebastian was sitting a distance away under a shady tree. He shook his head and sighed as he watched the little ones cuddle together to listen to Uncle Stumpy's story.

"Now, mates," began Uncle Stumpy, "me and the old master was asailin' the Caribbean when a most ferocious storm came out of nowhere. The sky blackened and the wind screamed and howled across the open sea. Waves as tall as the trees in the forest tossed our vessel about like leaves are blown before the wind. Yessiree, mates, I figured we was bound to end up in Davy Jones' locker that day, for sure. It took me and the old master both to hold the wheel. There was great waves on the right of us and there was giant waves on the left of us and there was massive waves crashing down on top of us." Uncle Stumpy paused a minute, then leaned forward and winked his eye. Clicking his teeth, he continued, "Then we

saw them lying before us in all their horrible ugliness."

"What did you see?" interrupted Rowdy.

"I'm gettin' to that, boy, just hold your horses," replied Uncle Stumpy. "Dead Man's Reef is what we saw, and many a good seaman has met his Maker because of those reefs. Well, anyway, our ship was tossed against the reefs. *Bang, slam* and *crunch* was the awful noise me and the old master heard as the reefs ripped holes in our ship. Now there we was, mateys, asinkin' in the storm, when the biggest wave you ever saw swept our old ship up and jammed it between two reefs."

"What happened then?" gasped Kadiddle Hopper.

Chuckling and pulling at his chin, Uncle Stumpy continued, "Well, mates, that's all that saved us from sinkin', was bein' hung up between those reefs. We just spent the evening and night hangin' there and waitin' for the storm to pass."

"Uncle Stumpy, what did you do when the storm passed?" asked Sassy.

"Oh, mateys, that's the most terrible part of this tale." Getting himself more comfortable on the log, Uncle Stumpy continued, "Sometime, way in the night, the storm passed. When the sun rose the next mornin', the sea was calm. Me and the old master thought the worst was over, so we went out on the deck to see what repairs would be necessary to get under way again . . . and there they was."

With his eyes widened in amazement, Rowdy asked, "What was there? What was there?"

"Octopuses was there . . . hundreds of them! A whole colony had been drug up from the bottom of the sea. There was little octopuses and medium-sized octopuses and large octopuses and giant, huge octopuses. There was octopuses on the reefs. There was octopuses all over the ship. They was on the left of us and they was on the right of us and they was in front of us and they was behind us! And they was all hungry and we was about to be their breakfast!"

"Oh, dear," gasped Patches, "what did you do then?"

"Wellsir, me and the old master drew our sabers as they attacked us. We chopped octopuses on the right and we chopped octopuses on the left and we chopped as they leaped through the air at us. And when we thought we had finally

whipped them back, the old granddaddy of all octopuses raised up out of the sea and, stretching forth one of his ugly tentacles, he snatched my trusty saber from my hand. Then down came another tentacle across my face and with one giant suction cup directly over my eye, he plucked my eye smooth out of me head in a split second."

"Oh, my goodness," gasped Sassy, "how terrible!"

"Yes," sighed Uncle Stumpy, "it is a terrible and frightening sight to see your own eye alookin' back at you from the bottom of an octopus' tentacle."

"Wh-wh-what happened then?" gulped Kadiddle Hopper.

"Wellsir," continued Uncle Stumpy, "old granddaddy octopus raised out of the water and summoned all of his grandchildren to his side and was about to devour us and our ship. Yessiree, mateys, we would have surely ended up in Davy Jones' locker that day if it hadn't a been for Robocoon. Yeah, old Robocoon came abustin' out on the deck with his machine gun arm blazin', and athrowin' fire from his eyes. He drove them octopuses off the ship, and ablazin' and shootin' at them out in the sea, he kept them drove back while me and the

old master made emergency repairs on our ship. Then we got unhung from them reefs and made our getaway from that nest of octopuses."

"Who and what is Robocoon?" asked Rowdy.

"Oh, mateys, you mean I haven't told you about Robocoon?" The little critters shook their heads. "Wellsir," said Uncle Stumpy, "me and the old master was docked in the Orient, and the old master met this curious Oriental fella that trades in unusual artifacts. Well, to make a long story short, he built Robocoon for the old master. The old Oriental used me as a model. Robocoon looks like a raccoon, but he is a robot. His left arm has a machine gun built into it, and just above his eyes is two small spouts that allow him to shoot flames out. He is fierce looking and a pure warrior."

"Is Robocoon with the old master now?" asked Rowdy.

"Ah, alas, Rowdy, it was so bad. The old master passed on to Davy Jones' locker a short time back. That's when I decided to come home to the forest. Just wasn't the same on the seas without him."

"Where is Robocoon, then?" asked Kadiddle Hopper.

"Wellsir, old Robocoon has stopped working. Something went wrong inside of him, and me and the old master didn't know how to repair him. Well, anyway, I took him apart and he is in my seabag in the old hickory."

"Wow! Neat!" exclaimed Rowdy as he jumped to his feet. "Can we see him?"

"You sure can," replied Uncle Stumpy. "Go, Rowdy, and fetch my seabag out here to me."

Rowdy rushed into the old hickory and drug the large seabag out. Uncle Stumpy opened it, and there lay Robocoon, all in pieces. Uncle Stumpy wagged his head and sighed, "My old friend, Robocoon, I wish I knew how to fix you."

Rowdy's eyes glistened as he said, "I know someone that I betcha could put him together."

Uncle Stumpy's one eye lit up with joy as he asked, "Who do you know, mate, that could do that?"

Rowdy related to his uncle all about King Benjamin, the Sagittarians, and particularly DC Bones. Rowdy and Uncle Stumpy agreed to go to the children's farm and ask Kevin to contact King Benjamin and request his help in repairing Robocoon.

Rowdy pulled his flying air scooter from its hiding place. Starting the air scooter up, he glided over to the log in front of Uncle Stumpy.

Uncle Stumpy rose to his feet and stumped his way around the air scooter to ask, "What manner of craft this be?"

Rowdy explained that it was a flying air scooter given to him by King Benjamin. "Hop on the back, Uncle Stumpy," said Rowdy, "and we'll go to the children's farm."

The old raccoon climbed on behind Rowdy, and *zoom!* they were off. Uncle Stumpy clung tightly to Rowdy as he shouted, "This be more sport than when me and the old master was ridin' wild kangaroos in Australia!" Dodging the trees, they sailed toward the old farm.

When they arrived, Rowdy introduced Uncle Stumpy to the children and told them all about meeting Woody the Wanderer. He asked Kevin to contact King Benjamin to seek his help in repairing Robocoon.

"Yes," said Kevin, "we need to talk with King Benjamin

anyway, because whatever is about to happen to our forest is close. Uncle Jim was very upset by a phone call he received this morning. He left immediately to fight against whatever the threat is."

Using the ring, Kevin contacted King Benjamin. He related to the king the young raccoons' request to repair Robocoon and told the king about Uncle Jim's trip.

"Yes," replied King Benjamin, "I've been informed that there's been an attempt to speed up the hearings in Austin. I believe it is time we discussed with you how you can assist us. I will send a flying platform for you now."

The children agreed to go to the Enchanted Kingdom for discussion. The king told them to bring the disassembled Robocoon and he would have DC Bones take a look at it.

Rowdy and Uncle Stumpy sailed away toward the old hickory to gather up the parts of Robocoon and wait for the air platform, while the children and Pete made their preparations to leave for the Enchanted Kingdom.

Chapter 4

The Threat

The flying platform arrived to pick up the children and Pete in the late afternoon. Making one more quick stop at the old hickory, a special messenger asked Sebastian to accompany them. The raccoons loaded the disassembled Robocoon on board, and the air platform streaked away toward the Enchanted Valley.

The air platform glided in by way of the Great Hall, and the passengers were greeted by Willard. He escorted them to the Inner Chamber, where King Benjamin met them.

Willard and DC Bones carried the disassembled parts of Robocoon into an adjoining room while King Benjamin escorted the little party into the Conference Room.

When all were seated, the king pulled down a large map on the wall and began, "My friends, your state government has proposed to build a huge nuclear power plant here — ten times larger than any in the world. If constructed, it will occupy thousands of acres of your forest and a part of our Enchanted Valley. In addition, many roads and houses will be built close by. Now, this problem is twofold. The first problem is that the roads, and traffic that would occupy them, would deface your beautiful forest, endanger your wildlife, and make

it impossible for us to remain in seclusion from the human population. The second and most important problem is the danger from nuclear waste. With all of the advancements humans have made in this area, there are still serious problems involved."

"What can we do?" asked Sebastian.

"Unfortunately," replied the king, "there is little the animal kingdom can do to prevent this. You must rely upon the good humans to protect your environment, which brings me to the subject at hand. Tommy, Kevin, Donna, your Uncle Jim is serving on a committee that is dealing with this problem. We hope that he realizes the seriousness of the situation and opposes it with great vigor."

King Benjamin glanced about the room, then replied, "We have studied your uncle a great deal and this is our evaluation of him. Number one — he is a good and honest man. Number two — he believes in protecting your environment and the animal kingdom's environment. Number three — he is a realist."

"What do you mean by 'a realist'?" asked Kevin.

"Well, Kevin," answered the king, "he knows the human population must have energy to heat and cool their homes and to run their machinery that makes the goods you enjoy. Now, Jim does oppose the nuclear plant being constructed here, but he realizes that it must be built somewhere. He is being opposed by another group headed by a despicable human named Norman J. Peabody. This man has bought up land in and around this area and wishes to sell it at a high profit."

"What can we do?" asked Donna.

"Your Uncle Jim is presently losing his fight to have the nuclear plant located elsewhere. So what we must do is supply him with facts on an alternative site where the animal population will not be disturbed."

"Do you know of another site?" asked Tommy.

"Yes," replied the king. Laying rolls of maps and documents on the table, he continued, "Our engineers have studied your state extensively and have found a desolate area where this plant could be built at a much lower cost, and it would not threaten any being's environment." Looking at

Tommy, he said, "Tommy, you are the oldest in your family. Will you give these documents to your uncle and ask him to study them?"

"I will," replied Tommy.

"Very well, we will be close by to help you convince him, if necessary." Pausing a moment, King Benjamin lowered his head slightly and sighed, "If the Light of Good is with us, possibly we can all maintain our worlds. Now I will have you all returned to your homes. We thank you with all our hearts for your concern!"

As everyone rose and started to leave the Conference Room, they heard an awful commotion coming from the adjoining room. Rushing in to see what was happening, they found DC Bones climbing on top of a tall cabinet, while Willard ran around the room with Robocoon in hot pursuit. Robocoon had taken Willard's staff and was poking him in the side as he ran.

Robocoon shouted, "You heathen lizard, you have robbed me of my weapons and I'll see you face the cat o'nine tails for that!" Seeing Uncle Stumpy enter the room, Robo-

29

coon stopped pursuing Willard and rushed to his friend's side. "Stumpy, my old mate, these heathens have stripped me naked and defenseless! Will you just look at me, Stumpy! My machine gun is gone and they've taken out my flame throwers! Who are these cutthroats we have fallen into the hands of?"

Uncle Stumpy was overjoyed that his friend, Robocoon, was working again. The old raccoon jumped about on his peg leg, slapping Robocoon on the back, and said, "It be all right, mate, these be friends we're among."

Willard, regaining his composure, approached the king, saying, "Your Majesty, DC and I examined this unit and decided he was far too violent in his present condition, so we removed his weapons of violence before we reactivated him."

Climbing down from the cabinet, DC stated angrily, "Yes, Your Majesty, and we tried explaining to this unreasonable thing that this is a peaceful place and he would not need his weapons."

"You tried to change my programming," interrupted Robocoon, "and make me a flower-carrying peacenik, and I'll not be standing for it!" He whirled about to face Stumpy and continued, "Stumpy, my friend, if this meek lizard and this massive ball of hair have their way, they will have me dancing on my tip-toes with a flower in my teeth! Please, please, Stumpy, don't allow this!"

"Now, now," said King Benjamin, "no one is going to tamper with your programming. And you may have your weapons back when you leave here."

King Benjamin instructed Willard to pack Robocoon's weapons in a box and return them to him. Willard did as he was instructed, and all journeyed down the long corridor to the Great Hall. As the guests boarded the flying platform, King Benjamin said, "Remember, Tommy, we will be close by to assist you in convincing Jim. Just present him with the documents and leave the rest to us."

The children, Pete, and raccoons waved goodbye as the flying platform sailed away to return them all to their homes.

Chapter 5

Uncle Jim's Promise

The Texas sky was tinted orange as the air platform sailed into the setting sun. Uncle Stumpy explained to Robocoon about the old master passing on. They sat in the rear of the flying platform, reminiscing about the adventures they had had together. Arriving at the old hickory, Robocoon and the raccoons left the air platform and waved goodbye as it headed toward the old farm. Darkness had closed over the old farm when Pete and the children arrived. Bidding the pilot farewell, they watched the flying platform zoom out of sight toward the Enchanted Kingdom.

"Come quick," said Pete, "I see Mister Jim is home." As the children entered the house, Uncle Jim greeted them with a hug and asked where they had been.

Tommy spoke up. "May I talk with you first, Uncle Jim?"

"Certainly."

They all gathered in the living room and Tommy asked, "Were you able to persuade the committee not to build the nuclear power plant here?"

Jumping to his feet in astonishment, Uncle Jim asked, "How do you know about that? No one is supposed to know!"

"Well," persisted Kevin, "are they going to build it

here?"

Uncle Jim paced the floor a minute and answered, "It will go before the state senate next week for a vote, but I'm afraid they will vote to build it here."

"Is it because Norman J. Peabody owns land here and can buy votes?" asked Donna.

"What?" exclaimed Uncle Jim, "how do you know about Peabody?" His pacing quickened as he continued, "You kids seem to know a lot about something that's supposed to be top secret. I think you had better explain where you got your information."

The children looked at each other a moment, then Tommy asked, "Will you believe us if we tell you? Will you give us your word not to reveal what we tell you?"

Uncle Jim resumed his seat in front of the children. Leaning forward, he placed his elbows on his knees and his chin in the palms of his hands and said, "I can't promise you that. If there is a leak in security, we must find the person responsible and remove him from office."

Looking Uncle Jim straight in the eye, Tommy stated, "I promise you that this information did not come from anyone in the office, or for that matter, from anyone of this world. But if you cannot respect our confidence, we cannot tell you."

After thinking this over, Uncle Jim replied, "Let me see if I understand the terms of our agreement. If the information didn't come from anyone who is of this world, then I must remain silent as to your source?"

"That is correct," replied Tommy.

"Very well, I agree," said Uncle Jim, chuckling a little.

Getting a very serious look on his face, Tommy reaffirmed, "You are giving us your solemn word?"

"Yes, I said I would," replied Uncle Jim. "Would you like to shake hands on it?" To Uncle Jim's astonishment, all three children rose, took his hand, and shook on his commitment. Leaning back in his chair, he admitted, "Well, this must be powerfully serious, so why don't you just lay it on me? I'm all ears."

Uncle Jim sat patiently and listened while the children told him all about the Sagittarians, the raccoons, and so on.

33

When they finished, he sat in silence, shaking his head. Finally, he said, "That's the most incredible story I have ever heard!"

"Do you believe us?" asked Kevin.

"I don't disbelieve you," replied Uncle Jim. "I am not sure what I believe at this moment. I must have time to consider it."

Tommy took the maps and documents that King Benjamin had given him and presented them to Uncle Jim, saying, "Please study these while you are deciding what to believe." Silence filled the room as they sat looking at each other.

Uncle Jim began to realize that he was wounding their pride by doubting them, so he said, "Even if all you tell me is true, you must realize, Tommy, that we have to have energy, and some sacrifices have to be made."

Tommy's voice quivered with righteous anger as he said, "Why don't you try telling Sebastian and Amanda that their children are going to be poisoned and that they must sacrifice? How would you like it if something were poisoning us and you were told to sacrifice?"

"Yes," said Kevin, "tell King Benjamin his people must leave their homes and go someplace else. They have never harmed anyone, and they saved my life in the storm. They don't have to sacrifice. They have the power to take our world from us and make us sacrifice, but they are too kind."

"Wait a minute, now," objected Uncle Jim, "you make me out to be a bad guy in this, and I'm not! I don't want it here, but there is no other place for it."

"Yes, there is," said Donna. "If you will study those papers King Benjamin sent, you will see. He said there was another site that would cost less to build it on, and nothing would be harmed."

Uncle Jim sat with his face in his hands for a minute, then said, "All right, you've made your point. I will study these documents carefully. If they prove to have a valid argument in them, then I will go back to the committee with a new recommendation."

The hour was growing late, so the children hugged Uncle Jim goodnight and prepared for bed.

Pete stood nervously twitching his hat in his hand. Uncle Jim asked, "Pete, did you hear what those children told me? What do you think about all of this?"

"Mister Jim," said Pete, "I tell you, the children are telling you the truth, and you'd best take them serious or all Hades is going to bust loose around here."

"You, too, Pete? Are you also against me?"

"No, the children are not against you. They are for you. They believe in you and your words. You have raised them and taught them to be full of goodness and truth, and that is what you are seeing come forth in them now. They will stand up and fight for what they believe is right. You, Mister Jim, of all people, should honor and respect this in them."

Nodding, Uncle Jim sighed, "I do, Pete. Believe me, I do."

Uncle Jim walked outside the old farm house and gazed at the stars as he reflected on all that had transpired.

Back in the Enchanted Kingdom, King Benjamin had observed all that had happened at the farm. He turned to Willard and asked, "Has Boo returned from the assignment we sent him on?"

"No," replied Willard, "he and the clerks you sent with him are still at the county seat, secretly photographing the land records of Norman J. Peabody."

"When they return, have them process all of the documents and bring them to the old farm. I am going there now to speak personally to Jim. He is indeed distressed as to what to do. Perhaps we can help him understand the options he has."

"Do you wish for me to go with you?" asked Willard.

"No, Willard, just have a flying platform sent to the Great Hall. Use the Oracle to contact Woody the Wanderer and request that he meet me at the old farm in one hour."

"As you wish," replied Willard.

While King Benjamin boarded his flying platform, Uncle Jim had gone back inside the house. Laying the documents on his desk, he prepared to retire to bed. As the moon rose slowly into the night sky, Uncle Jim fell fast asleep, unaware of the extraordinary experience he was about to endure.

Chapter 6

Uncle Jim and the King

The stars glistened and twinkled in the night sky while all at the farm fell fast asleep. The flying platform arrived carrying King Benjamin and an escort of Woolly Bees. As it came to rest in front of the farm house, the children's two dogs, Charles and Samantha, bounded up to greet their friend, the king.

The little reddish-brown cocker spaniel, Samantha, excitedly wagged her bobbed tail and said, "Oh, gosh, it is so good to see you. We have been away in Austin so much recently, staying with relatives of Master Jim's. We have missed out on so many things going on here."

The black schnauzer, Charles, pranced about and asked, "What brings you here at this hour, Your Majesty?"

The king briefly related his mission to them and asked which room Uncle Jim was sleeping in.

Raising his paw, Charles pointed to the open window on the second floor, then stated, "My good fellow, if you are going into the house, be extremely careful. Pete's large, fat cat is sleeping somewhere about and just might mistake you for a tasty midnight snack."

As the king thanked them, a brilliant turquoise ball appeared in the sky and lowered to the ground in front of them. A voice spoke from the glowing ball: "I am here, Benjamin, what do you wish?"

The king described his wishes to Woody and Pywacket. He wanted them to use their power of illusion to show to Uncle Jim, in vivid pictorial scenes, the desecration to the forest and wildlife that would follow construction of the nuclear power plant.

"This is a simple enough task," replied Woody.

The king showed Woody the open window and asked him to take a position in Jim's bedroom and wait. The turquoise ball rose slowly to the open window and disappeared inside the room.

Two Woolly Bees flew to the front door. Using a special key DC Bones had prepared for them, they quickly unlocked and opened it. The king scurried inside the old farm house and made his way to the winding stairs that led to Jim's bedroom.

As he crept up the darkened stairs, the king carefully searched the shadows for Pete's large cat, Pussywillow. *Ah*, he thought to himself, *Pussywillow is probably in the kitchen. That is where the food is and that is his favorite place.* He began to bound and leap up the remainder of the stairs. But to his sudden shock, he came face to face with Pussywillow, who was napping at the head of the stairs.

"Uh-oh," said the king as the cat's large eyes popped open. Their faces were just inches apart. "Now, pussycat," said the king calmly. Pussywillow frowned and his long, pink tongue slithered out across his freckled nose. The cat slowly rose to his feet, his eyes glaring down at the little king standing in front of him. As the king slowly backed up, he said, "Now, now, Pussywillow, let's talk about this."

The cat slinked forward and, crouching, said, "I don't know what you are, but you are just in time to fill an empty spot in my stomach."

"Egads!" exclaimed the king. "That will be the day!" He whirled about and jumped down the stairs, shouting, "Somebody get this beast!" As the king reached the bottom of the stairs, he could feel the cat's hot breath on his back. He

quickly dashed under a small footstool as Pussywillow crashed
head-on into it.

The cat reached his huge paw up under the stool, swat-
ting and trying to nab the little king. He said, "Oh, now, come
on out. I don't want to hurt you. I just want to eat you."

Woody had heard the king's shouts of distress and glided
the turquoise ball out of the bedroom and down to where the
cat was attempting to snag and pull the king from beneath the
stool. Pussywillow saw the turquoise ball floating beside him
and slapped at it.

Woody created an illusion. The turquoise ball turned
into a huge, vicious wolf. With teeth bared, the wolf snapped
at the cat. Pussywillow's back bowed up and his hair stood on
end as he saw the vicious wolf. Abandoning his quest to catch
King Benjamin, Pussywillow ran through the open front door
and into the night, squalling in terror.

The illusion of the wolf vanished, and once again the turquoise ball was floating about the stool as King Benjamin
crawled out of his hiding place. Woody was chuckling from inside the ball as the disturbed little king dusted himself off. As

he stood looking at the turquoise ball and listening to Woody laughing from inside it, he also began to chuckle.

Charles and Samantha burst through the front door to see what had happened. They had puzzled looks on their faces, observing the floating ball and the king, and hearing hearty laughter from both.

The king exclaimed, "Now, wouldn't that have been the most degrading end for the Supreme Ruler of the Sagittarians — to end up in the belly of a lazy old, fat cat!" Regaining his composure, the king said, "Well, now, let's get on with our business."

Accompanied by the floating ball, he climbed the stairs and entered Uncle Jim's room. Leaping upon the bed and upon Uncle Jim's chest, he declared, "Wake up, Jim, my boy."

"Huh? Who is there?" mumbled Jim, still half asleep.

"It is I, King Benjamin, and I have come to speak with you on a matter of concern to both of us."

"Oh, all right," sighed Jim as he snuggled down in bed and dozed off to sleep again.

Hearing Woody's chuckle from the ball that was now floating up in the corner of the room, King Benjamin said, "Well, this may be more difficult than I had originally thought." He leaped to the pillow beside Jim's head and, using his knuckles, rapped on Jim's forehead. "Is anybody in there?"

"Uh-huh," said Jim as he reached over and turned on the lamp beside his bed. Seeing the little king standing on his pillow, he exclaimed, "Holy Moses!"

"No," replied the king as he paced about on the pillow, "I am not Moses. He was a man far greater than I. I am simply King Benjamin, Ruler of the Sagittarians."

"Oh, no . . . no," said Jim, "I didn't mean you were . . . ah . . . well, ah. Oh, never mind. Who are you anyway?"

The little king scratched his head for a second, then replied, "I must be getting old, because I thought I just told you who I was!"

"Oh, no," said Jim as he put his face in his hands, "you must be a nightmare brought on by those wild stories the children told me or those greasy enchiladas Pete fixed me tonight."

"No, no," replied the king, "I am not something you ate, although your cat almost ate me awhile ago."

With his hands still covering his face, Jim peered out between his fingers at the little king standing on the pillow. "What do you want?"

"Well, Jim, my boy, I want you to take a little trip with me and my friend," said the king, pointing to the glowing ball.

Jim's eyes widened as he stared at the turquoise ball floating in his room. "What is that?"

"That is Woody and Pywacket. They are Illusions, but that is of no matter at the moment," replied the king. "You will receive no harm from us or them."

Jim, now wide awake, said, "Well, if this is a dream, it is certainly very real. If it's not a dream, then my curiosity as a newspaperman compels me to accompany you and learn." Leaping from his bed, he quickly dressed and inquired, "Where are we going?"

"On a little trip," said the king. He went to the open window and motioned for the flying platform. The platform rose and hovered alongside the open window. With a little bow and a wave of his hand, the king said, "Be our guest."

As Jim climbed through the window and onto the platform, Woody asked, "Benjamin, why didn't you come in the house this way? You wouldn't have had such an ordeal with that cat."

King Benjamin shrugged his shoulders as he boarded the platform and replied, "I didn't think about it."

Jim glanced around the platform at the curious-looking Woolly Bees and asked, "Who, or maybe I should ask *what*, are they?"

"They are Woolly Bees," answered the king.

"Oh!" Jim managed to say.

With everyone on board, the airship sailed into the night toward its destination.

"Where exactly are we going?" asked Jim as he uneasily settled back for the ride.

"We are going to give you a close-up look at where your state government intends to build its nuclear power plant. We

will allow you to see it before and after they build it."

"What do you mean, see it after they build it?"

The king pointed to the turquoise ball moving alongside them. "Woody and Pywacket are going to use a special talent they possess, to show you in detail what to expect if the power plant is built here."

"Oh," said Jim, "that will be interesting . . . I think."

Soon they arrived at the proposed site, and the airship rose high enough to allow them to observe the entire area. Jim looked down on the forest and the Enchanted Valley, glistening in the moonlight, and remarked, "How absolutely beautiful!"

"Now," said the king, "Woody will show you the change."

Suddenly it was daylight all around them. Before them stood a huge nuclear power plant, belching its smut into the air. There were poisoning pools of water around it. Roads sprawled out in all directions, defacing the beauty of the wildlife preserve. In another instant Jim's mind shifted and moved in for close-ups. He saw that there was an absence of the usual abundant wildlife. He saw, in his mind, animals wailing for the loss of their paradise. He saw suffering from sickness among some of the animals that once flourished and enjoyed the clean environment of the forest. He heard the cries and moans of the animals for their dead. He saw the sadness of King Benjamin's people, having to leave their beautiful valley.

"Enough, enough," protested Jim, "I have seen enough." The illusion passed and he gazed once again upon his beautiful forest, sprawling beneath him in the moonlight. "I do not want this plant here, but I face powerful and influential men who support its construction here." Jim turned to the little king and continued, "I am losing this fight to Norman J. Peabody. He heads the group that supports this site. He has a great deal of money and power in this state."

"Yes," said the king, "and if my suspicions are true, he has bought up land around this area and intends to profit excessively from this."

Slamming his hand down on the rail of the air platform, Jim said, "If I could only prove that, I might swing enough votes to defeat him."

The king smiled and said, "By the time we return to your home, you may just have the proof you desire."

Jim's eyes lit up as he replied, "I certainly hope so."

The king thanked Woody for his assistance. Woody bade them farewell, and in an instant the turquoise ball vanished into the sky.

The air platform turned about and sailed swiftly toward the old farm as Jim said to King Benjamin, "Every newspaperman dreams of being just where I am now."

"What do you mean?" asked the king.

"Well," replied Jim, "here I am sitting in the middle of one of the hottest stories to hit this planet."

"You mean, a nuclear power plant is of that much interest to the human population?"

"No," chuckled Jim, "I mean, alien beings from another world living right under our noses for a couple of thousand years or so, and we are not even aware of their existence! This story would surely win me a Pulitzer prize and fame and fortune in my profession. It is every newspaperman's dream. But to print it I would have to break a solemn promise to the children."

"What will you do?" asked the king. "Will you print it and break your commitment to them?"

Jim paced about the flying platform for a minute, then answered, "As important to me as the recognition, fame, and fortune that would surely come with it, there is one thing that is a thousand times more important."

"And what is that?" asked the king.

Smiling, Jim said, "The love and respect of the children. So, no, King Benjamin, your people's secret is safe. I will honor my commitment to the children and remain silent about your valley. But I do want one commitment from you."

"What is that?"

"When your people decide to make themselves known to this world, I want the story," replied Jim.

"Jim, my boy, you've got a deal," stated the king.

As they arrived at the old farm, they found Boo the Bat waiting for them with copies of land documents from the county seat. Uncle Jim quickly examined them and discovered Norman J. Peabody and his associates had purchased lands under dummy corporations and were selling them to the state at a huge profit.

Clutching the documents tightly, Jim exclaimed, "I will fry Peabody's fat, little rump with these. This evidence you have brought me, along with an alternative site, just might weaken his support."

"Well," said the king, "they will be of help. Now I'll return to my kingdom and if you need any further assistance, the children know how to contact me." The king paused a moment, then continued, "On behalf of myself and my people, please allow me to express our deep appreciation for all your efforts on our behalf. We are grateful for your concern, regardless of the outcome."

As the king started to depart, Jim said, "Wait just a minute, please. There is still one piece of unfinished business between us."

"Oh," queried the king, "and what is that?"

Standing beside the platform and looking the king in the eye, Jim said, "The most precious things in the world to me are the children. They have become my life." Pausing for a moment to contain his feelings, Jim continued, "Kevin informed me last night that one of your people — I believe it was some kind of lizard, acting under your instructions — saved his life in the storm. I have not thanked you for that, so please allow me to express my deepest gratitude for preserving this precious life."

As the two honorable beings from two separate worlds gazed at each other, there was no need for further words. The king raised his hand in a sign of peace as his airship sailed away into the night.

As the first sun rays flickered across the tops of the trees in the forest and danced about on the walls of the old farm house, Uncle Jim was pacing the floor. He was studying the maps, figures, and documents supplied to him by King Benjamin.

The children came downstairs for breakfast and saw the documents scattered all about the living room. Donna asked, "Have you been up all night?"

44

"Not all night, but most of it," replied Uncle Jim.

"Will the papers we gave you help?" asked Kevin.

"They certainly will," replied Uncle Jim.

With his head lowered a bit, Tommy asked, "Do you believe us?"

Uncle Jim laid the documents down and said, "Come, children, sit." The three little ones sat on the couch in front of their uncle. Looking affectionately at them, Uncle Jim said, "Last night I should have had every reason to believe you and none to disbelieve you, but sometimes we all make mistakes. Last night I made one by doubting the ones closest to me. Will you please forgive me?" Uncle Jim stood humbly before them, waiting for their response.

The children jumped from the couch and into the arms of their uncle, saying, "Yes, yes, yes!"

Pete had been standing in the door of the kitchen, nervously twisting a towel in his hands as he watched this scene. He exclaimed, "Well, by golly, old Pete will fix a big breakfast now and we will all enjoy!"

As they all sat about the breakfast table, Uncle Jim announced that he had to leave for Austin in a few moments, to organize a fight against Peabody.

"May we go into the forest today?" asked Kevin.

"You certainly may go into our beautiful forest," replied Uncle Jim, "and I promise you, Kevin, that I will wage one heck of a fight to see that it remains beautiful."

Charles reared up on Kevin's chair and asked, "Can Samantha and I go with you?"

Kevin, cocking his head back and imitating Uncle Jim, said, "You certainly may go into our beautiful forest with us."

Uncle Jim laid his napkin down on the table and asked, "Did you and the dog just have a conversation?"

"Yes, we did," replied Kevin.

"Uh . . . uh," stammered Uncle Jim, "did the dog speak to you and did you understand what he said?"

"I certainly did," Kevin said with a grin on his face.

Uncle Jim's eyebrows rose a little as he stated, "That's remarkable!" Glancing at the dog and then at the children, he continued, "And when you go into the forest do you speak

with and understand your little raccoon friends and other animals?"

The grin widened on Kevin's face as he replied, "Yes, we do."

Uncle Jim leaned back in his chair, clasped his hands behind his head, and said, "That is truly incredible!" Smiling and shaking his head, he continued, "King Benjamin told me that you children had noble and pure hearts and possessed a special gift, but I had no idea it was this special."

Tommy leaned across the table and excitedly exclaimed, "You met King Benjamin?"

"Oh, yes," chuckled Uncle Jim, "he visited me last night and fully explained the situation. Oh, by the way, Pete," continued Uncle Jim, "you need to do something about your cat. Pussywillow almost ate King Benjamin last night."

Clapping his hand across his mouth, Pete groaned, "*Aaah!*" Snatching a broom, he swatted the fat cat, who was napping by the refrigerator, and said, "You bad Pussywillow! You almost ate His Majesty!"

Pussywillow slipped and slid about the kitchen floor, attempting to dodge Pete's broom. He finally made a quick exit out the back door and headed toward the safety of the barn.

As Uncle Jim prepared to leave for Austin, he said, "Tell your little raccoon friends that I would like to meet them, and that I will do everything in my power to preserve their forest."

As the children stood on the front porch and watched Uncle Jim drive away, Tommy remarked, "Doesn't he look like a knight going out to do battle?"

Leaving the dishes to Pete, the children hurriedly prepared their things and, along with the dogs, scurried down the hill and into the forest to find their friends.

Chapter 7

Mike and Grady

Venturing into the forest a short distance, the children and their dogs arrived at the old hickory and described to the raccoon family the story of King Benjamin's visit to Uncle Jim, and how their uncle was going to lead a fight against Peabody.

Robocoon stated, "If Stumpy will give me my weaponry back, I will make short work of this pirate named Peabody."

Stumpy slapped his buddy, Robocoon, on the back and said, "My old shipmate, this forest is a place of peace. While we are here we shall remain at peace."

The children expressed a desire to meet Woody the Wanderer. Charles and Samantha were fascinated by Uncle Stumpy and decided to stay behind and listen to him spin yarns.

The three children and raccoons ran into the forest to search for Woody. After searching the forest for a while, they rested in the shade of a large, bushy tree. As Rowdy leaned back against the trunk, he noticed something hiding in the dense foliage above.

"Who's there?" shouted Rowdy.

"*Sssh,*" said a voice from the foliage, "we're hiding."

Jumping to his feet, Rowdy picked up a large stone and demanded, "You'd better come out of there so I can see you, or I'm going to chunk you out!"

"Don't chunk, we're coming out," replied the voice.

The foliage moved a moment, then out flew Grady the Eagle and Mike the Hawk. Both flew to the ground in front of the children and raccoons.

"Well howdy, Grady, Mike," said Rowdy, "what are you hiding from?"

Stretching his wings and strutting, Grady said, "We are hiding from Hattie and Attie."

"You mean the two large Owl sisters?" asked Rowdy.

"Yeah," replied Mike.

Rowdy scratched his head a minute, then asked, "Well, why are you hiding from them?"

Hopping about on the ground, Grady said, "It's — it's all Mike's fault. I mean, it was his idea!"

"Wait a minute," protested Mike, "I wasn't the one that led them on!"

Rowdy chuckled and asked, "What did you say to them, Grady?"

The eagle shook his head and replied, "Well, I, uh, don't know exactly what I said. You see, they live in Farmer Magruder's barn. It's full of all kinds of good grain, and they know how to get into the grain bins. And, well, Mike gets this idea that if we were sorta nice to them, that they might share some of their delicious grains with us."

Mike the Hawk jumped in front of Grady and said, "What I said was, 'sorta be nice to them.' You, Grady, strutted around and flirted with them and they got the wrong idea about what our intentions were!" The hawk raised his wing, pointed at the end of the eagle's beak, and continued, "I was just quietly eating some grain when you, Hattie, and Attie strolled out by the pond. When ya'll came back, old Hattie was aflutterin' and aflirtin' all around me and making goo-goo eyes. What did you say to them?"

"Uh . . . well . . . well, uh," stammered Grady, "I guess I just sorta mentioned maybe how lonely you were."

"What!" exclaimed the hawk.

"Well, uh, I mean . . . you know, uh . . . I don't remember all I said. I was thinking about all that lovely grain and I must have sorta, maybe, gotten carried away. But Mike," continued Grady, "you put me up to it, remember that. You put me up to it!"

"Well, this is a fine mess you've gotten us into," replied Mike. "Those two Owl sisters have been stuffing themselves on grain for the past two years and have gotten almost as large as the barn they live in, and now they are after us!"

"Well, uh, I'm sorry, Mike. I just wasn't thinking about that at the time. I was only thinking about the grain."

By this time the raccoons and children had burst into laughter, watching and listening to the eagle and hawk attempt to blame each other for their predicament. All the laughter had attracted the attention of the two Armadillo brothers, Marvin and Arvin. The two colorful Texas armadillos usually knew all the latest gossip in the forest.

As they strolled out of the underbrush, Marvin said, "I be needin' a good laugh, too. What bein' so funny?"

Sassy described to the Armadillo brothers the situation

Grady and Mike had gotten themselves into with the Owl sisters.

"Ha, ha, ha," laughed Arvin, "so you bein' the ones that them gals' pappy be atalkin' about!"

"Whatcha mean, whatcha mean?" asked Mike.

Marvin strolled up to Grady and Mike and said, "Them gals' pappy, old Harv, he be talkin' about weddin' bells aringin' in the forest."

"Yeah," added Arvin, "and he be atalkin' about matrimony, but we no be aknowin' until now who bein' the lucky grooms."

"Oh, my gosh, my gosh," nervously exclaimed Grady, "what are we going to do?"

Mike stood stunned, with his beak hanging open. Then, slamming his beak shut, he raised his wings into the air and screamed at Grady, "What did you promise them? I am in the prime of my life! I am too young to get married! Particularly to one of those homely Owl sisters! Either one of them, Grady, is bigger than the both of us put together!"

Just as Grady was about to answer, they heard a cry from

above, "Yoo-hoo! Yoo-hoo! There you are, little sweets."

Looking up, they saw the two large Owl sisters descending out of the sky toward them. *Kerplunk!* Hattie landed. *Kerplunk!* Attie landed.

"Oh, oh, oh me," giggled Hattie as she fluttered around Grady.

Attie waddled over by Mike and, giggling, said, "Papa Harv wants to see y'all."

Mike swallowed loudly before asking, "Wh-wh-what does Papa Harv want with us?"

Sassy saw the embarrassing situation Mike and Grady were in. She did not wish to see the Owl sisters' feelings hurt, so she decided to, temporarily, get Mike and Grady off the hook. "Grady, I believe it is time for you and Mike to go and see our papa about the threat to our forest. He might even want you to go to the Enchanted Valley for him."

"Oh . . . oh yes," replied Grady, "I had almost forgotten about that."

The Owl sisters fluttered about, giggling and batting their eyes at Grady. "Oh, how wonderful you are! And how brave to help defend our forest!"

The flattered Grady cocked his head back, poked his chest out, and strutted around a minute. "Yes, we must do our duty to protect you fair ladies of our forest."

Tapping his claw on the ground and frowning at Grady, Mike said, "You are getting us in deeper!"

Grady blinked his eyes, then said, "Oh, oh yes, I see what you mean." Continuing, he said, "We must excuse ourselves now."

Mike hopped over to Sassy and said, "Sassy, dear, you are a sweetheart and a princess. Thank you so very much."

Both birds leaped into the air. As they flew into the sky, the raccoons and children saw Mike fly close to Grady and pop him with his wing. The children and raccoons chuckled over the birds' antics.

"Rowdy, where you be aheadin' now?" asked Marvin.

"We are looking for Woody the Wanderer," replied Rowdy.

"Oh," said Marvin, "I be hearin' about this here Woody,

and me and ol' Arvin would like to be ameetin' him too. Would you be amindin' if we be acomin' along with ya'll?"

"We wouldn't mind at all," replied Rowdy.

They said their goodbyes to the Owl sisters, Hattie and Attie. As the little group resumed the search for Woody, the Armadillo brothers chuckled between themselves about the predicament Mike and Grady had gotten into.

Marvin laughed. "Ha, ha, ha, did you see how ol' Mike and Grady abein' nervous and asweatin' and asquirmin' when Hattie and Attie be afindin' them?"

"Yeah," replied Arvin, "but I be havin' a feelin' they no bein' half as nervous as they gonna be when ol' Pappy Harv acatches up with them two young scalawags!"

"Whatcha reckon ol' Pappy Harv agonna be adoin' to those boys?" asked Marvin.

"I don't be aknowin'," replied Arvin, "but I wouldn't want to be astandin' in their feathers now that ol' Pappy Harv be atakin' into his mind to be amarryin' the girls off."

Chapter 8

Woody's Assistance

As the little group approached Skull Waterfalls, they saw their friends, Woody and Pywacket, sitting on a log, visiting with Leaper Frog and Needles Porcupine.

Rowdy turned to the children and said, "That's Woody, but be careful what you ask him or he will have you going up and down, in and out, back and forth, and all around the subject."

Sassy introduced the children and the Armadillo brothers to Woody and Pywacket. The Armadillo brothers looked the curious Woody over and imagined all the wonderful stories they could tell throughout the forest about their experiences with him.

Woody heard their thoughts and said, "I am all you believe and much more, and since you both receive a special delight in sharing knowledge with the other animals of the forest, I shall treat you to an extraordinary experience. It will surely give both of you a special tale to spin." With that statement, Woody created an illusion and the Armadillo brothers were suddenly way out in space, riding inside a capsule. They could see the beautiful planet Earth beneath them. It appeared to be about the size of a basketball.

"Oh my," exclaimed Marvin, "how it be we gettin' way out here?"

"I not be aknowin'," replied Arvin, "but I be awonderin' how we be agettin' back!"

Then, without warning, the capsule took a nosedive straight for the Earth. The two bewildered and terrorized armadillos clung to each other, eyes bugged out, as Arvin said, "I doubt if this abein' such a good idea!"

"Yes," replied Marvin, "I not bein' sure it bein' worth this to have a good tale. Maybe we should not abeen havin' such a curiosity about this Woody!"

"Yeah," agreed Arvin, "maybe we should abeen stayin' behind with the Owl sisters and not abeen abotherin' this here Woody fella."

The capsule came very close to the Earth, leveled off, and orbited the planet. It soared at tremendous speed as Marvin and Arvin delightfully observed many lands, peoples, and critters around the entire world.

As suddenly as the illusion began, it ended. The two Armadillo brothers stood before Woody, gazing at each other in disbelief.

Woody chuckled and said, "Well, that should keep you busy sharing your experiences with the other animals of the forest for a while."

"It sure enough bein' more than me and ol' Arvin had bargained for, but in the future if'n it bein' all right with you, we'd just as soon you'd be atellin' us things than ashowin' us." The Armadillo brothers excused themselves and trotted away into the forest to share their extraordinary experience with all who would listen.

Woody gazed at the children and said, "King Benjamin has chosen you to defend the interest of the youth of this world and to safeguard the welfare of the animals of your forest from the desecration of an environmental threat."

"What do you mean?" asked Tommy.

Woody smiled, "Think for a moment about the kind of world you would like to grow up in and about the plight of the animals, and I will show you how I will assist you at the proper time."

As Tommy and the others thought on the subject, Woody created an illusion for all present to share in.

When the illusion passed, the children and raccoons exclaimed, "That was so real!"

"Yes," replied Woody, "and we will do the same thing before your state senate. King Benjamin and your uncle will explain all this to you."

The children and raccoons spent some time visiting with Woody, and he demonstrated how illusions of the future would help.

It had grown late in the evening and was time for everyone to return to their homes. Bidding Woody and Pywacket a farewell, the raccoons left for the old hickory. Taking Charles and Samantha, the children returned to their home.

At the old farm, the children found Uncle Jim had returned. He was quite excited about the support he had gained against Peabody. "We still have an uphill fight, but at least we now have a chance." He asked the children if they would take the raccoons with them and address the state senate just before the vote on the nuclear power plant site. The children said that they would.

"Fine," said Uncle Jim, "now visit with the animals of the forest. Get their feelings written deep in your hearts so you will speak with knowledge and power. Then the three of you prepare a presentation. I will take you to Austin in three days and you will address the senate."

The old farm buzzed with excitement as the children planned their address. It was agreed that they would get up early the next morning, go into the forest, and learn all they could from the animals.

At the first light of day, the children got up and dressed hurriedly. They packed a picnic lunch and scurried away to the forest. Arriving at the old hickory, they told Sebastian all about their going to Austin and asked if Sassy, Rowdy, and Patches could accompany them.

Sebastian thought about it for a few minutes, then replied, "I don't know where Austin is, but I assume it is a long distance from our forest. I trust you and your uncle to watch over and keep them safe, and if it will help protect our forest, then I suppose it will be all right."

The children related to Sebastian that they intended to spend the entire day in the forest, getting to know the animals' feelings about their home.

Sebastian asked, "Would it be helpful if you were able to address all the animals at one time?"

"Yes," replied Kevin, "I believe that would be very helpful."

"Very well," said Sebastian, "I will call a meeting for sundown at Digger Doug's cavern." Saying goodbye, Sebastian immediately went into the forest to notify all the animals about the gathering at Digger's at sundown.

The children and raccoons said goodbye to Amanda. As they were about to leave, Uncle Stumpy said, "Me and old Robocoon would be obliged if you mates would allow us to cruise with you today."

"Why not?" replied Tommy.

With that, they departed the old hickory and ventured deep into the forest in search of truth and understanding. Little did they know that another group, headed by Peabody, was also investigating the forest.

Chapter 9

Peabody and the Gators

The children and raccoons moved deeper into the Big Thicket. The air became still and humid as they approached the swamplands. Having a special sense of awareness this day, they allowed their hearts to be more sensitive toward the beauty of their surroundings.

As they slowly made their way along one of the waterways that feed the swamp, Rowdy stopped suddenly and said, "Listen!"

"What do you hear?" asked Sassy.

Rowdy crouched low and stared at the edge of the water and said, "Something is moving along beside us in the water." Taking a long pole, he swatted the water and shouted, "Come up out of there so we can see you!"

First, two eyes popped up above the water. Then two more eyes popped up. Finally, two more eyes appeared.

"It be crocodiles!" shouted Uncle Stumpy. "Run for your lives, mates!"

"Don't run, Uncle Stumpy, it's just the Gator sisters, Shawna, Debbie, and Tina," said Rowdy. "They are alligators and they won't hurt us. They are our friends."

"Well, blow me down!" stammered Uncle Stumpy.

"Friendly gators! Now I've seen everything."

All the alligators crawled out on the bank. Shawna said, "Good morning, Rowdy."

"What brings you down here, and who are your friends?" asked Debbie.

Sassy introduced everyone to the friendly gators and described to the Gator sisters the threat to their wilderness.

"Goodness," said Tina, "I hope you can prevent this, because we do not wish to see our lovely swamps destroyed."

As the little group sat and visited with the three alligators, they heard, in the distance, human voices coming their way. Taking cover in nearby bushes, they observed four humans approaching.

Three of the humans were carrying cameras, instruments, and barrels of something. Leading the group was a man about five feet tall and almost as wide. Rolls of blubber hung over his belt. His face was as round as a plump Texas watermelon but nearly as red as a strawberry, and he had a small goatee.

Robocoon peered through the bushes. "Thar she blows, mate, old Moby Dick hisself!" he exclaimed.

"Sssh," said Tommy, "let's listen and see who they are."

One of the humans carrying a camera shouted to the fat man, "Mr. Peabody, is this far enough into the forest?"

The children's and raccoons' eyes grew large and round as they got their first look at their adversary, Norman J. Peabody.

Peabody answered by saying, "I guess this will do. I want film and still shots, and I want you to make it look bad. I don't know what that meddling newspaperman is up to, but when he tries to convince members of the senate of this forest's beauty, I want to show them a wasteland."

"But Mr. Peabody, this is not the site where they are going to build the nuclear power plant. It is very beautiful where they are going to build it."

Waving his arms and shaking his head, causing his fat cheeks to bounce, Peabody replied, "That doesn't matter. The senate doesn't know that. And by the time, if ever, they learn, it won't matter. The plant will be under construction. I will

have my money and nobody will dare oppose me."

"Do you know them?" whispered one of the Gator sisters.

Donna quickly and quietly explained that this was the person who wanted to pollute and destroy their forest.

Tina raised her head and frowned. She said, "Shawna, Debbie, do you smell a plump lunch out there?"

As the little group huddled and quietly whispered a plan to each other, Peabody shouted instructions to his crew. "Dump that oil and toxic waste at the edge of the swamp and do close-up shots that make it appear as if the entire area is polluted — a contaminated wasteland, fit for neither humans nor beasts." Pulling a handkerchief from his pocket, he wiped the sweat from his face and sat upon a large stump. He sneered, "Jim is a fool. I offered to cut him in on this and he spouted off about protecting the wildlife and the youth of America and the world. I tell you," he continued, "he is a bleeding-heart environmentalist, but I'll squash him like a cockroach when he tries to oppose me. I'll smash him under my feet."

Tommy burst from the bushes and shouted, "That might not be as easy as you think. You might just find my uncle a little bit hard to step on!"

"Huh? What?" Peabody jumped to his feet. "Who are you?"

Robocoon said to the Gator sisters, "If I had my flame-thrower still in me, I would treat you to barbecued blubber for lunch."

Kevin quickly exclaimed to the others, "Tommy has stuck his foot in it for sure now. We had better move quickly to back his play."

Robocoon nudged Stumpy. "Mate, I smell a good fight in the brewing out there."

Tommy walked slowly but proudly toward the glaring Peabody. Pounding his fist on his chest, he said, "I am Tommy, and the man you think you can squash is my uncle."

"Ho, ho, ho," mocked Peabody, "you're just one boy! I could have my men take care of you here and now."

Kevin bounded out behind Tommy and said, "Make that two boys."

63

They were quickly joined by Donna, who said, "No, two boys and one girl."

Rowdy pulled his slingshot from his hip pocket, placed a large stone in it, and drew aim on Peabody.

Peabody waddled around the stump a minute, then said, "There are still only three of you. And if I want it, you could disappear in these swamps and never be heard of again." Peabody pulled at his goatee and glared at the children. "Maybe you should just go home now and forget what you have seen and heard here."

"Never!" declared Tommy. "You are faking evidence, and if you try to use it, we will expose you for the greedy fraud you are!"

Peabody studied the children for a minute, then decided to try to frighten them into silence. He threatened, "There are quicksand pits all through this swamp, and you just might accidentally fall into one of them." Then, with mean and evil looks on their faces, Peabody and his men moved toward the children.

Shazam! Rowdy let the stone fly from his slingshot and it struck Peabody squarely on the end of his wrinkled red nose.

"Ouch!" cried Peabody. "Get them!"

With that statement, the battle was on. Robocoon grabbed a long stick and dashed toward Peabody like a knight charging a dragon.

"Oouff!" yelled Peabody as the stick jabbed him in his pudgy belly.

Using the stick like a sword, Robocoon struck Peabody on his chubby little legs and shouted, "You blackhearted pirate! I'll run you through!"

The children defended themselves with sticks and swung at the approaching men. Rowdy, Sassy, and Patches leaped through the air, landed on the shoulders of the men, and bit and scratched them fiercely in an attempt to protect the children.

While Uncle Stumpy hopped toward Peabody, he saw his little robot shipmate take a kick from Peabody. The little robot coon sailed through the air, end over end. Uncle Stumpy took one giant leap and landed astraddle Peabody's

neck.

Using his peg leg, Stumpy flailed Peabody about the head as he shouted, "If it be war you want, it be war you get, you slime of the sea!"

While the children and raccoons struggled with the men, Peabody pulled Uncle Stumpy from his neck and slammed the old raccoon down on the large stump, causing Uncle Stumpy's peg leg to stick in the stump like a dagger.

As Uncle Stumpy hopped up and down on the stump, trying to pull his peg leg free, he exclaimed, "Now that be the lowest skulduggery, dirty trick you be pulling yet!"

Peabody looked around and saw a large club. As he bent over to pick it up, he screamed in pain, *"Oowwee oooo!"* as Shawna Gator sank her sharp teeth into the seat of his pants.

The three men saw the other two alligators charging at them and shouted, "Gators! Run for your life!"

Throwing the raccoons from their shoulders, they turned and ran in terror as Debbie and Tina Gator snapped at their backsides. Following close behind them, Peabody waddled, ran, and screamed as Shawna Gator held tightly to the seat of his pants.

At last, Shawna released her bite and allowed the terrified Peabody to join his men as they fled from the area.

Robocoon made his way out of the bushes and rushed to Uncle Stumpy to help him unwedge his peg leg from the stump. The Gator sisters rejoined the others as they laughed and discussed their experience.

Thanking the Gator sisters for their help, the little group again made its way toward Digger Doug's cavern for the meeting. They spent several hours roaming the forest and sharing the ideas of the animals as they continued slowly toward Digger Doug's.

As they followed a small trail past some fallen trees, a familiar voice called out to them, saying, "Howdy, Rowdy, Sassy, Patches."

Looking around, Rowdy saw Shawn, the Horny Toad, sitting on the trunk of one of the fallen trees.

The little group approached the toad and Rowdy inquired, "How's everything going for you, Shawn?"

The little horny toad blinked his eyes and replied, "Oh, pretty good, I guess. I'm like a one-legged critter. I can't kick."

Uncle Stumpy limped over to the toad and declared, "Now look here, toad, that ain't funny!"

The little toad saw that Stumpy had only one leg and replied, "Sorry, meant no offense."

"Well, then, none taken," replied Stumpy.

"Where ya'll going, Rowdy?" asked the horny toad.

"To Digger Doug's cavern for a meeting of all the animals."

"Oh," replied the toad, "I would like to go, but ya'll move too fast for me to keep up."

"Want to ride on my shoulder?" asked Donna.

"Sure would, honey, if you don't mind me coming along." Donna put her hand out and Shawn scurried up her arm to her shoulder. Looking at the children, he said, "I wish all humans in Texas were as friendly as y'all are."

As they began once again toward Digger's, the little toad asked, "Is the old badger, Digger Doug, still digging for

gold?"

"Yes," replied Sassy, "he is still trying to dig out enough gold to buy a human."

"What?" exclaimed Donna.

"Yes," replied Patches, "he thinks if he gets enough gold he can buy a human, because his old grandpappy told him many years ago that for enough gold, some humans would sell themselves."

"Well, I hope he doesn't take it into his head to buy us," replied Donna.

Rowdy chuckled a minute, then said, "You know, it wouldn't be a bad idea if Digger could get enough gold to buy Peabody, and then make him sweat some of his blubber off working in Digger's mine."

They all laughed heartily as they approached Digger Doug's cave.

Chapter 10

The Understanding

Some of the animals had already gathered as the children and raccoons arrived. Rowdy bounded over to his friend, Digger Doug, and said, "Hi ya, Digger."

"Well howdy, Rowdy," replied Digger. "Shucks, I ain't seen you and the girls since ya'll gave that musical show for all the critters." Looking over Rowdy's shoulder, Digger saw the children and exclaimed, "Are these the humans what are looking out for us?"

"Yes," said Rowdy, then introduced them.

Donna looked at the old badger and said, "I'm not for sale!"

The old badger placed his hand across his mouth and chuckled a bit, then replied, "Well, shucks, that's a right shame, 'cause I'd love having a critter as cute as you around here."

At last all the animals arrived and Sebastian called the meeting to order. He introduced the children and turned the meeting over to them.

As the children stood before the animals, they saw the turquoise ball floating in the corner of the cavern and realized that Woody was there to create an illusion in the animals' minds. That way they would better understand the children's words concerning the dangers from a nuclear power plant, since most animals do not comprehend the awesome power and destructive force of nuclear energy.

Tommy was the first to speak. "My little friends, our state government intends to build a huge nuclear power plant. This plant is ten times larger than any in the entire world and will spread over thousands of acres of our forest."

As Tommy spoke, Woody showed the animals, in an illusion, the meaning of these words.

The animals sat spellbound as Tommy continued, "Now, it is necessary for this plant to be built to supply growing energy needs to the human population. However, it is not necessary to build it in your beautiful world."

Kevin added, "King Benjamin has supplied documentation on an alternative site for this plant at a lesser cost to our state. The site King Benjamin proposes will not pose as close a threat to the environment."

Donna then took her turn. "Our Uncle Jim is leading a fight against a greedy and selfish man named Peabody, to persuade the state to choose the alternative desolate site. My brothers and I are going to Austin with our uncle in two days to plead your cause before our state senate."

The children gazed around at the little animals who looked bewildered and frightened. Woody had revealed to their minds the full danger this plant represented to their world.

Tommy continued, "We need your help. Tell us what is in your hearts so that we may understand and present your case with all the knowledge and power possible."

Slick the Weasel Lawyer stepped forward and held out toward the children his law book entitled *Texas Wildlife Rules and Regulations*. His voice trembled as he said, "This book is a collection of your human laws that protects us from excessive harm. I have believed in it and that humans were bound to abide by its rules. Now, are you telling us that humans will not honor its words?" A small tear slipped from the corner of the weasel's eye as he continued, "Since the beginning of time, the humans have always been more intelligent than the ani-

mals and have ruled over the animal kingdom. They have said they wish to protect their world and ours. Are they now saying they no longer care about our world?"

Kevin looked at the saddened and disillusioned Slick and replied, "Nuclear power can be good for all if harnessed and controlled. But Slick, it is not just your world that can be threatened by its misuse. Our world can be destroyed too." Kevin paused a minute while he looked into the faces of all his friends, then continued, "The humans who wrote this book believe in its contents, but they face a continuous struggle with selfish and greedy humans who only want what they can obtain for the moment, without considering the harm to others."

Digger Doug humbly stepped forward and said, "I have been working for many years, digging out gold and saving it, but I will give them all of my gold if they will not hurt our forest."

One at a time, the animals came before the children, clutching their families. They unselfishly offered all their possessions to the human population if it would help the other animals preserve their forest.

The animals' words and feelings burned deeper and

deeper into the hearts and minds of the children until, at last, all had spoken. In all the days of the Big Thicket never had there been such an atmosphere of unselfishness, love, and consideration for each other as on this night.

As the children stood in the harmonious atmosphere of generosity and benevolence, the Light of Good burned as brilliantly as a fire inside them. Donna said, "You have given us your hearts and your feelings. We will carry your cause and ours before our state government and present it with all the power and might we can."

Sebastian adjourned the meeting and the children moved out among the animals and visited them for a while before time to return home.

As the children bade the animals farewell and started their journey toward home, the animals did not leave the children. Instead, they gathered around the children and walked with them through the forest.

At last they reached the edge of the forest and could see the old farm. The animals huddled together and watched the children walk up the field toward their home. Seldom ever have human hearts grown as much as the children's did that night. As they glanced over their shoulders, they could see their little animal friends cuddling together in the moonlight, waving an affectionate goodbye.

Chapter 11

A Trip to Austin

Uncle Jim greeted the children as they entered their house. "Was today a learning experience for you?" he asked.

"Yes," they replied, and they described to Uncle Jim their encounter with Peabody and their meeting with the animals.

The children spent most of the next day preparing for their address before the state senate. Late in the afternoon, Sassy, Rowdy, and Patches arrived to spend the night with the children since they were all to leave at dawn for the trip to Austin.

As night fell, the children prepared small beds for the raccoons and all retired early. As they lay in bed with the thoughts and hopes of tomorrow on their minds, sleep crept up on them.

The rooster crowed loudly, announcing the breaking of the day as the smell of eggs and pancakes drifted into the bedrooms. The cool morning breeze gently lifted their curtains as it drifted through the windows. As the children hurriedly dressed, they realized at last it was here — their day of confrontation with Peabody's forces. This day would decide the future of their beautiful forest.

After a quick breakfast, the children, raccoons, and Uncle Jim placed their things in the car and departed for Austin. As they all looked one last time at the beautiful forest behind them, they understood the importance of this day.

The little raccoons marveled at the curious sights outside the world of their forest as they passed through many cities and small towns. It was about midmorning when they arrived in Austin, the capital of Texas. As they drove up the long street toward the state senate, excitement abounded in their hearts. The children carried the raccoons on their shoulders and enjoyed the sights while Uncle Jim entered the chamber of the state senate to see when they were scheduled to be on the docket. Peabody's forces were busily presenting their cases and making last-minute lobbying efforts to hold their votes.

It was lunch time when Uncle Jim returned to the children and said, "The senate is adjourning for lunch. They have heard all the evidence on both sides. The votes are close and it could go either way. You children will address the senate after lunch, then they will vote."

Uncle Jim escorted the children and raccoons to a nearby restaurant for lunch. Entering the restaurant, they saw Peabody and his associates gorging themselves at a long table.

Peabody saw Jim, the children, and raccoons enter. In a loud and insulting manner he remarked, "Does this restaurant allow smelly and filthy animals in it?"

Rowdy whispered in Tommy's ear, "Can I jump in his face and poke him in the eye?"

"Easy," said Tommy, "easy. Uncle Jim will deal with him."

The manager, a longtime friend of Uncle Jim's, approached and asked, "Jim, do you have a good reason for bringing the animals in here?"

Uncle Jim replied, "I do. They are evidence in a senate hearing, and we have no place to leave them where they would be safe from certain persons."

"I understand," said the manager as he seated them.

Uncle Jim and the children ordered their food while Peabody continued to heckle them. Tommy leaned over and whispered to Uncle Jim that Rowdy wanted to punch Peabody.

Uncle Jim chuckled a minute, then said, "Children, I want you to understand that violence is seldom the answer to a problem. It is written in a most precious book that he who is slow to anger is greater than the mighty."

"What do you mean?" asked Kevin.

"Well," explained Uncle Jim, "a man who is in control of his temper can usually think things through and seldom makes a mistake in the heat of the moment. He is in control of the events taking place around him. But someone who loses his temper easily will lose control of himself, and he is controlled by the events that are taking place around him."

As they attempted to enjoy their meal, Peabody continued to laugh and make snide remarks loudly enough for all to hear.

After they finished their meal, Uncle Jim thanked his friend, the manager, and prepared to leave. As he passed close to Peabody's table, Peabody called out, "Jim, please come here for a moment. I have something to ask you."

Uncle Jim walked over to Peabody. "What do you want?"

Peabody laughed loudly while he rubbed his large belly. "I always thought you were very smart. Do you really intend to have those raccoons in the senate chamber? And do you think you can defeat me by having some snot-nosed, impudent, brat kids address the senate?"

Uncle Jim stood for a moment, looking at this obnoxious human, then replied, "You, Peabody, care for nothing but your own greed. Those children care for all, even you. And yes, I do intend to defeat you. I will leave you to feed your fat, greedy face now." Uncle Jim started to turn away, then stopped and added, "It is a shame you won't be able to enjoy your mashed potatoes."

"Oh, why not?" asked Peabody arrogantly.

"Because of that blob of ugly fat in them," said Jim.

"Huh?" Peabody looked into his plate. "What blob of ugly fat?"

Uncle Jim put his hand behind Peabody's head and pushed Peabody's fat face into the plate of mashed potatoes and gravy and said, "Your *face* is what blob of ugly fat!"

Taking the children by the hands, Jim walked proudly out the door as Peabody snorted mashed potatoes out of his nose and shouted, "We'll see who wins!"

Rowdy was extremely happy and jumped about on Tommy's shoulders as the children and raccoons walked toward the senate chamber. Donna eased up to Uncle Jim and said, "What was that about 'slow to anger,' 'greater than the mighty,' and controlling your temper?"

Uncle Jim cleared his throat and said, "I shouldn't have done that, and I am very ashamed that I allowed my anger to get out of control."

"Oh," said Kevin as he looked his uncle in the face, "you don't look ashamed. You look very pleased with yourself."

Uncle Jim cleared his throat again. As a blush of embarrassment came across his face, he replied, "I guess there are times when you've just got to do what you've got to do!"

The children and raccoons sat outside the senate chamber and waited to be called. At last the moment was at hand. They were called to address the senate. Walking down the aisles past the honorable senators, they reached the podium. There they were introduced by the president of the senate. They looked first at each other, then at their Uncle Jim, standing close by. Searching the ceiling, they saw the floating turquoise ball and knew that Woody and Pywacket were there to assist them.

Calling on all of his courage and feelings, Tommy began, "It is an honor and privilege to be allowed to address the elected representatives of the great state of Texas. Please allow me to introduce our raccoon friends. We call them Sassy, Rowdy, and Patches. They live in an old hickory in the Big Thicket. It is they, and all animals who enjoy a clean and wholesome environment, who are threatened by the construction of the nuclear power plant. It is also the world of the youth of tomorrow that might be endangered if you do not protect their environment. You may well endanger your own children's world of tomorrow."

Woody and Pywacket scanned the mind and heart of each senator present. Understanding what each was sensitive to, they began to reveal to the senators mental pictures to ac-

STATE OF TEXAS

company the words that flowed from the children. As the children took turns speaking, the senators were caught up in the powerful feelings and emotions in the words.

Concluding their address, the children thanked the senators for their time. As they walked proudly back down the aisles, the senators rose and applauded them. Once outside, they sat anxiously awaiting the results of the voting.

To the children and little raccoons, it seemed like an eternity before Uncle Jim bounded through the door. Leaping into the air, he shouted, "*Ooweee!* We won, we won!"

While they were dancing around with joy, a not-so-happy Peabody stormed out of the chamber, growling, "What am I going to do with all that land I bought?" He stopped, looked at Uncle Jim, and said, "Bleeding heart newspapermen! Emotional children! Loving animals! What is this world coming to?" Grumbling, he shook his head and stomped away.

"Oh," said Donna, "we must hurry home and tell the animals and King Benjamin and his people."

Kevin nudged her and said, "They already know."

"How?" asked Uncle Jim.

Kevin pointed to the window and said, "Look!" They saw Boo the Bat peering in with both crossed eyes, grinning and waving his wing at them.

As the senators came out of the chamber, they shook hands with Jim and the children. The senate president said, "Jim, those kids have a future in politics. Never have I heard an address given that came with such vivid mental pictures and force."

The children smiled as they walked to the window and saw Boo and his air bubble and Woody and Pywacket and their turquoise ball disappearing into the sky.

Chapter 12

The Honor

As Uncle Jim, the children, and raccoons journeyed toward home, they received an unexpected visit from King Benjamin. His sparkling image appeared before them in the car.

Standing on the dash, he held his arms open and said, "My heart is full. Our people are grateful. We are your friends, and we shall always be your friends. Our messengers are spreading the word of victory throughout the forest. Sebastian and I will prepare a victory celebration tonight to honor you. If it is acceptable to you, a flying platform will be awaiting you at your farm when you arrive. It will take you to a special place in the forest so that we may express our gratitude to each of you." His sparkling image faded.

It was almost sundown as they arrived at the old farm. There they found a special flying platform awaiting them as King Benjamin had promised. Pete and the dogs, Charles and Samantha, rushed out into the yard to greet them.

Pete exclaimed, "Ah, Mister Jim, it is so wonderful! All the little animals are safe! All the little people of His Majesty's world are safe!"

The honor guard from the Enchanted Kingdom closed ranks around them and escorted them to the special flying platform. It was all decked out in glorious colors, including three flags. The Texas state flag was on the left. The Enchanted Kingdom flag was in the middle, and the United States flag was on the right. When all were aboard the gloriously arrayed platform, it rose and sailed into the forest. Darkness gathered around them, and long before they reached the designated place, they could hear the music and joyous jubilation of the victory celebration. When they arrived, they were all caught up in the beauty of the scene. Beings from the Enchanted Kingdom had lighted the entire area with all manner of colored and curious lights. All the beings in the Enchanted Kingdom and all the animals of the forest were present as the airship lowered gently to the ground in the midst of this collection of glorious creatures.

King Benjamin greeted them and addressed Uncle Jim, "Allow me to present you with this ring," and he slipped the ring on Uncle Jim's finger.

Uncle Jim was pleasantly surprised. He could now hear and understand what the animals were saying. This was truly delightful as he listened to their conversations for the first time. Jim stood on the platform in amazement and looked out at Woody and Pywacket and into the faces of all the animals and all the different kinds of beings from the Enchanted Kingdom. As he and the children stepped from the platform, a rousing cheer from all present rang through the night air.

The next couple of hours were spent in joyful merry-making as musicians from the Enchanted Kingdom provided musical entertainment. Everyone enjoyed dancing, singing, hugging, and exchanging expressions of great joy. They feasted upon a banquet of fruits and vegetables and drank all manners of tasty nectars.

As Rowdy danced about, he accidentally bumped into his old adversary, Slick. He knocked Slick's glass of berry nectar all over the weasel. Rowdy's eyes bugged out as he said, "Uh-oh!"

The weasel stood with the nectar dripping off the end of his nose, smiled and said, "No, no, you will not upset me tonight. It is too magnificent a night to allow even your mischievousness to spoil it." Then, raising his finger, he chuckled and said, "But look out tomorrow, boy. Just you watch out for me

on all the tomorrows to come!"

The beautiful Texas moon rose slowly over the forest. Its soft, radiant light shone on the joyous group below as the richness of human kindness mixed with the loyalty and devotion of the animal kingdom. It was now woven and bound together by the honorable beings from another world. They would all work in harmony to create many wonderful and exciting adventures in all the days that lay ahead. The wind sang in the treetops, and all was well. Peace and joy were upon the Earth.

From the Author

Sassy & Rowdy express the good and fun-loving nature that is in so many of our hearts.

We hope you have enjoyed reading this adventure of Sassy & Rowdy, and that you are looking forward to reading all their books.

We welcome your comments on this book and would like to extend an invitation to the young and young at heart to submit your ideas on adventures for Sassy & Rowdy.

Address your letters to Sassy & Rowdy at P.O. Box 1883, Denton, Texas 76202. Sassy & Rowdy will personally answer your letter.

Now Available

Episode 1	The Adventures of Sassy & Rowdy (The Enchanted Valley)	$9.95
Episode 2	The Adventures of Sassy & Rowdy (Gory Gary Strikes Back)	$9.95
Episode 3	The Adventures of Sassy & Rowdy (Danger in the Big Thicket)	$9.95

Mail orders to:

EAKIN PRESS
P.O. Drawer 90159
Austin, TX 78709-0159